UPSIDE DOWN
AND
INSIDE OUT
Poems For All Your Pockets

Bobbi Katz

HOW I GOT TO BE A PRINCESS:
AN AUTOBIOGRAPHICAL NOTE

Yesterday my friend said,

"You look just like a princess."

I could not believe him.

Was he talking to someone else?

I looked behind me

and

in front of me.

I looked under the bed

and

on top of the closet.

No one else was there.

Again my friend said,

"You look just like a princess."

He really said it to ME!

I felt all twinkling inside.

That's how I got to be a princess.

UPSIDE DOWN
AND
INSIDE OUT
Poems For All Your Pockets

by
BOBBI KATZ

Illustrated by
WENDY WATSON

WORDSONG

BOYDS MILLS PRESS

Published by Wordsong
Boyds Mills Press, Inc.
A Highlights Company
910 Church Street
Honesdale, PA 18431

Publisher Cataloging-in-Publication Data
Katz, Bobbi.
    Upside down and inside out: poems for all your
pockets / by Bobbi Katz ;
illustrated by Wendy Watson.
[48] p. : ill. ; cm.
Originally published by Franklin Watts, New York, 1973.
Summary: Poems that spark the imagination of young children.
ISBN 1-56397-122-4
1. Children's poetry, American. 2. Humorous verses--Juvenile
literature. [1. American poetry --Collections. 2. Humorous verses.]
I. Watson, Wendy, ill. II. Title.
811 / .54 --dc20   1992
Library of Congress Catalog Card Number: 91-68197

The text of this book is set in 14-point Souvenir.
The illustrations are done in pen and ink.
Distributed by St. Martin's Press
Printed in the United States of America

10 9 8 7 6 5 4 3 2 1

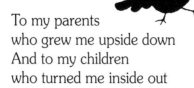

To my parents
who grew me upside down
And to my children
who turned me inside out

UPSIDE DOWN AND INSIDE OUT

Upside down and inside out,
Come, let's turn the world about!
Let us play when it is night.
Let us sleep when it is light.
Let us splash without our boots.
Let us pick a flower's roots.
Let us make the big things small.
Let us make the littles tall.

We'll wear mittens on our feet.
Boxes, bags, and jars, we'll eat.
We'll go skating, when it's hot.
We'll go swimming, when it's not.
We'll ask horses in for tea,
Not a lot, just two or three.
Upside down and inside out,
Come let's turn the world about!

GROWN-UP-DOWN TOWN

In a special town quite far away,
the kids are ten feet tall,
and all the grown-up people
are not very big at all.
They have to call them something else
in this special town.
The grown-ups are so little,
they call them grown-up-down.

The kids make all the rules there,
and here is something new!
The grown-up-grown-down people
do what they're told to do.

Sometime on a vacation,
I would so much like to go
to the town where kids are bigger
than the grown-up-downs, and so—
since my daddy has a road map,
and he could find the way,
I hope that he stays home from work
so we could go today!

WHY

Why do things have to be
1-2-3 and A-B-C?
It would be more fun to say
3-2-1 and C-B-A!

A BAD CASE OF COMMAS

In Alphabet City, where letters reside,

The problem is commas, washed up by the tide.

They're into the spelling that all letters do.

They've wiggled their way into words, sad but true.

They're hanging on H's. They're snoozing on Y's,

And some of them bumped the dots off the I's.

They're bungling B's. They're troubling T's,

And several of them have popped open the P's.

The problem is dreadful. The problem is bad.

The problem is driving the A,L,P,H,A,B,E,T MAD!

SCHOOL, SOME SUGGESTIONS

If kids could be the teachers,
If kids could make the rules,
There'd be a lot of changes made
In almost all the schools.
First thing they'd stop the homework.
They'd never give a test.
They know that growing children
Must have their proper rest.
They'd make the lunchtime longer—
Let's say from twelve to two,
So every growing boy or girl
Had time enough to chew!

Of course, concerning recess,
Kids clearly realize
To keep his body healthy,
A child needs exercise.
And so there would be recess,
Perhaps from nine to ten,
And then when it is two o'clock,
It's recess time again!
With longer, stronger weekends,
Each child would grow so smart
He would perform with excellence
In music, gym, and art!

A MATH LESSON

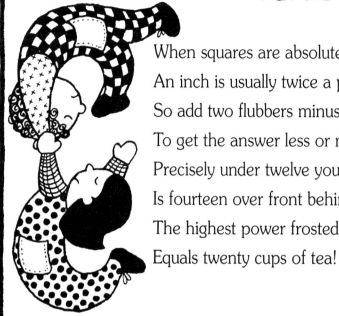

When squares are absolutely round,
An inch is usually twice a pound.
So add two flubbers minus four
To get the answer less or more.
Precisely under twelve you'll find
Is fourteen over front behind;
The highest power frosted three,
Equals twenty cups of tea!

To check your answer just proceed
The problem backward with great speed:
Tea-ish, me-ish, frosted three-ish,
Front-behinder, fourteen-finder,
Less-ly, more-ly, flubber-fourly,
Poundish, roundish, squarish, soundish.
Math as you can hardly see,
Is easy as a bumblebee!

A SONG TO SING TO YOUR MOSQUITO BITES

One and a two
and a scritchy-scratchy screw.

Three and a four
got a scritchy-scratchy more.

Five and a six
and a scritchy-scratchy fix.

Seven and an eight

Scritchy-scratchy feels so great.

Nine and a ten

Scritchy-scratchy them again!

JUMP ROPE JINGLE

Applesauce and alligators,
Blueberry pie,
Pickles in your pocket,
Cupcakes in the sky.

Swing on a seesaw,
Sing like a crow,
Slip on a sunbeam
Tied in a bow.

Stringbeans and lollypops,
Spaghetti on a tree,
Wherever fish have feathers,
The popsickles are free!

THINGS TO DO IF YOU ARE A SUBWAY

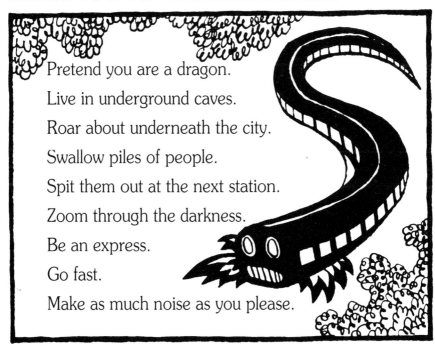

Pretend you are a dragon.

Live in underground caves.

Roar about underneath the city.

Swallow piles of people.

Spit them out at the next station.

Zoom through the darkness.

Be an express.

Go fast.

Make as much noise as you please.

THINGS TO DO IF YOU ARE A FLOWER

Be a wonderful color, like purplish pink.

Stay out in the rain.

Understand what the wind says.

Dance to its rhythms.

Grow toward the sun.

Smell good.

Give bees honey.

Count every star.

Be beautiful.

THINGS TO DO IF YOU ARE THE SNOW

Dance, dance, dance all the night.

Fly in the sky—

Cover all the streets—

Cover all the grass—

Pile up on the rooftops—

Perch on the branches of all the trees—

Sparkle when the sun shines—

Quiet the city.

Close the schools!

THINGS TO DO IF YOU ARE A PIZZA

Get started by a man who wears a white hat.

Get stretched and pulled and thrown in the air.

Get shaped in a circle,

Sprinkled with cheese,

Slurped with sauce,

Slipped in an oven.

Sizzle.

Bubble.

Watch out! Someone will eat you!

THINGS TO DO IF YOU ARE A COLD

Attack some nice kid.

Tickle his throat.

Disappear his voice.

Give him two days off from school.

(Sniffle, sniffle, sniffle.)

Get drowned in rivers of orange juice

And chicken soup.

Be a pest.

Disappear!

THINGS TO DO IF YOU ARE A STAR

Twinkle
and
Twinkle
and
Twinkle
and
Twinkle
and
Twinkle

RECIPE

I can make a sandwich.
I can really cook.
I made up this recipe
that should be in a book:
Take a jar of peanut butter.
Give it a spread,
until you have covered
a half a loaf of bread.

Pickles and pineapple,
strawberry jam,
salami and bologna
and half a pound of ham—
Pour some catsup on it.
Mix in the mustard well.
It will taste delicious,
If you don't mind
the smell.

CURIOUS QUESTIONS

Have you ever seen a fish that walked?

Have you ever heard a grasshopper talk?

If you ask me how I know that they do,

I'll hop on one foot and say

Doodle-dee-doo!

Have you seen a tomcat reading a book?

Do you know a walrus who skates on a brook?

If you ask me how I know that they do,

I'll hop on one foot and say

Doodle-dee-doo!

Have you seen a hippo who danced on her toes?

Did you meet a horse in a store buying clothes?

If you ask me how I know that they do,

I'll hop on one foot and say

Doodle-dee-doo!

Have you seen a fox blow a jazz clarinet?

Have you heard a duck quacking, "Don't get me wet!"

If you ask me how I know that they do,

I'll hop on one foot and say

Doodle-dee-doo!

PRETENDING

When you are in bed and it's cold outside,

do you ever pretend that you have to hide?

Do you curl up your toes?

Do you wrinkle your nose?

Do you make yourself little so none of you shows?

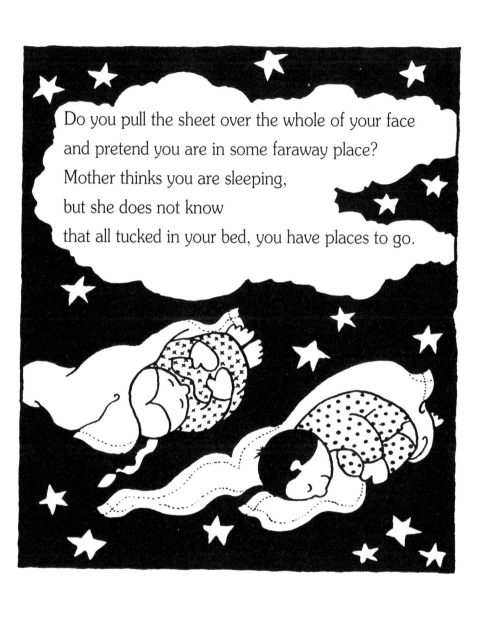

Do you pull the sheet over the whole of your face
and pretend you are in some faraway place?
Mother thinks you are sleeping,
but she does not know
that all tucked in your bed, you have places to go.

IF

If we could sit on tables,
and eat our food off chairs.
If bears had tails like monkeys,
and monkeys growled like bears,
your dad could be your mother,
your mom could be your dad,
and you'd get piles of presents,
whenever you were bad!

A RESOLUTION

Someday I am going to go

To a T.V. studio.

Someday I am going to see

All those people who look at me!

SOMEDAY

Don't you wish that you could say
you are your mom or dad someday?
Then you could tell your parents stuff
like maybe they're not clean enough?

Sure, you could say, "It's time for bed,"
when they would rather play instead,
or when they want hot dogs to eat,
Pass the spinach!
Pass the meat!

Yes, it would be such fun, if say,

you were your mom and dad someday,

and they might learn a lesson, too,

when all the orders come from you!

ADVICE: HOW TO CHOOSE A PET

A puppy-cat or pussy-dog
Will make the nicest pet,
But if you cannot locate one,
Try not to get upset.
Look for a flying hamster
Or a gerbil that can sing.
A parakeet with bunny ears
Might be the very thing.

Perhaps you'll find a goldfish
Who will bark and sit and heel.
Just avoid the sort of creature
Who might want you for a meal!

COMPANY

I'm fixing a lunch for a dinosaur.

Who knows when one might come by?

I'm pulling up all the weeds I can find.

I'm piling them high as the sky.

I'm fixing a lunch for a dinosaur.

I hope he will stop by soon.

Maybe he'll just walk down my street

and have some lunch at noon.

I'm baking a cake for a garter snake
with sand and a bucket of glop.
You never know when a garter snake
might wiggle up and stop.
I'm baking a cake for a garter snake.
It's best to be prepared.
Because when I meet a garter snake,
I'm always a little bit scared.

TRAVEL PLANS

If you could go anywhere, where would you go?

Deep in the jungle? Deep in the snow?

Deep in the ocean to talk to a fish?

If you could go anywhere that you could wish—

If I could go anywhere, here's what I'd do:

I'd pop in the pouch of a kind kangaroo.

I'd travel around for as long as I please,

And learn to say "thank you" in Kangarooese.

I'd make myself little and then I would see
The part of a flower that interests a bee,
The way the world looks from the tail of a kite,
The way the birds sleep in their nests in the night.

I'd go through the hole in a needle, like thread.
I'd spin like a top on the point of my head.
I'd skate on an ice cube. I'd swim in a glass.
I'd talk to a grasshopper, if any should pass.

And when I got tired of being so small,
I'd ABRACADABRA myself to be tall!
I'd step over oceans. I'd step over seas.
I'd cause a few shipwrecks, if I had to sneeze.

I'd pet a giraffe on the top of his head.
I'd find out for sure, if the North Pole was red.
And when I had seen all that I want to see,
I hope I'd know how to turn back into me.

MORNING

It's morning in the afternoon,
so eat your bacon with a spoon.
And if you have a scrambled egg,
you could feed it to your leg.

Then drink your milk up with your nose
and hop right into daddy's clothes.
Put your left shoe on your right.
It's time to start the day.
Good-night!

THE ARTIST, THE AUTHOR, THE BOOK

Wendy Watson can stand on her head,

while stirring the jam pot or kneading the bread.

Harrah for our artist! "It's nothing," says she.

"Father Fox gave me the recipe."

Bobbi Katz swung too long on a swing.

That mixed up the way she sees everything.

While her two kids grow up, she's growing down.

She builds her friend mountains all over town.

These two zany ladies decided one day

that life would be more fun, if seen their way.

Together they made this little book.

Just close your eyes and take a look!